SHOWER FROWN
by

Ro bin Mountjoy
WGAE, (c) July 4th
2008
edited by
Ruth Kennedy-Mountjoy

Characters

Andre Waykoff, Landlady's boy toy / Mimi Rodington, l andlady/

Ralph Ozzie, Mimi's tenan t/
Renay Kent, College girl / Joe
Ness. Musician / Tamera
Jackson, Tow lo t receptionist
/ Lilly Smiles, Girl lost and
confused at tow lot / Trish
Dunbar, Employee of Finneli's
Fine Funerals / Pat Samson,
Guard at tow lot / Captain
Mondo , Captain of the tow lot

ACT 1
SCENE 1

Time: 6:30am
Setting: Summer of 2006 / New York,
New York. The bedroom of Mimi and
Andre's apartment a glamour shot of
Mimi is proudly displayed on a table
next to Andre.

At Rise: Andre is lifting dumbbells.
He is wearing a bathrobe.
ANDRE

Sets down the dumbbells grabs
picture admiring it as h e turns
 talk to the audience

(He has a Russian

accent.)

ANDRE

I have known Mimi for a few weeks
now. When I arrived in America with
my old girlfriend, Sasha, who was
to start studies at the university,
we needed a place to stay. I called
this number I saw on a poster
flier. That is how I meant

Mim i

the first week we arrived. Me and
Sasha moved in than a week later
Sasha runoff .
(pause for beat)
I'm heartbroken she left me
nothing. I do not understand. Why
she would leave? Then I found out
from Mimi that Sasha had been
frolicking with a Dominican named
Carlos. I don't know what I'm going
to do now.
(S adly)

ANDRE
Ohh the motherland nothing more
than a mamory for me now.

MIMI
Enter stage left, apartment bathroom.
Grabbing Andre's mouth and squeezing it.
MIMI
That's memory, say it memory nothing
more than a memory.

A NDRE
Memory, thank you, nice for
you to help me with my English.
M IMI

Just like Sasha a memory.
ANDRE
I just can't believe she did this
to me.

MIMI
Well it's ok baby just move her
stuff down to the basement she ran
off with the dirty druggie peddler!
So put her stuff in
the incinerator that way there
will be no more memory of whats her
name. No more, not even one.

A NDRE
Yes you are right I have been
betrayed it is true so there shall
be revenge.

MIMI
They left the country I overheard
them talking about going to the
Dominican Republic.

ANDRE
Ohh what to do? what to do? I'm a
man without a home! A man without
a country. My heart is cracking
left by my Sasha. Why?

M IMI
I told you when you two moved in
that she was trouble! I could just
tell, you know I have my ways of
sniffing out trouble makers.

A NDRE
It does not make sense we where to
be married in the fall.

M IMI
I've seen this before darling.
Married in the fall this simply
won't be happening after all.

MIMI
For as you know she has fallen,
into the arms of another man.

A NDRE
(SAYS WRONG WORD FOR BROKEN SAYS TOKEN)
Ohh my, my heart is token. What am I
going to do? Where will I go? I can
not afford to live in this country
alone. The rents are like sky high
rocket's!
M IMI
You know there are a few things
around the building that need
fixed. I could work something out
for you, since you seem so pathetic
and heart broken. yes that's it, you
do some work around the building

for me and you can stay rent free.

A NDRE
You would do this for me?

M IMI

I'm sure we could work it out.
ANDRE
What type of work?
M IMI
Ohh you know a little maintenance,
running a errand here and
there, grab the groceries laundry
things like that. For as you know I don't
like to go
outside it's so dirty out there.

Yes and besides, I've always wanted
my very own white Russian. Sip sip
a little nip hear and there sounds
pretty tasty to me.

A NDRE

What do you mean you want some
vodka to make your white Russian.
Want me to go and get ?

M IMI
No I Have a job for you .

ANDRE
But I don't have any tools.
MIMI
This job only requires one tool.

Mimi grabs Andra by the crotch and
pulls   him   into   her   arms   then

throws him on the floor and they
start going at it the lights fade.
M IMI
Ohh Andrea you can stay in my room
with me!

A NDE
Mimi,Mimi,Mimi,Mimi,Mimi,Mimi,Mimi,
M IMI
No Andr e m e!
Lights fade

Act 1

S cene 2
Time: 10:30 am

S etting: Mimi alone in the
living room. big trash bag on
floor and mop

At Rise: Cleaning talking to
herself and six months have
passed.
MIMI
My Andre fills my bed up like a big
old Russian bear. I'm able to rent out our
 extra room
it's nice you know, but it's just
that it's just so difficult to find
good tenants nowadays .

M imi starts to s ing.
This is the way we wash are floor,
we wash our floor, this is the way
we wash the floor early in the
morning.

Oh, the swiss and their watches

don't burn so well. I'll have
to mail this to them. Those two
tenants were so dirty.

Well there not going to be
cluttering up my place anymore
goodbye, Mr.,and Mrs. Johanson.
One more bag of nasty
into the incinerator.
How a couple like the Johanson's
could just up and run off leaving
so much junk in their room is
beyond me!
Bad people bad!
Bad people can't stay with me
running off leaving all this crap
behind!

Now I have to do my rounds its
that time of the day. Ohh so much
to do clean the new vacant room
get ready for my next lovely
couple. I didn't really see any reason for
the Johanson's to up and leave without
even saying goodbye. That's just
rude. They won't be getting back
there deposit that for sure leaving
such a mess behind!
Hopefully the next tenants will be
better looking an hopefully just a
tad bit more polite and clean.

I kinda like my Andre
Mr. Johanson's could not compete
with my Andre he's just too small.

Not like Andra big and beautiful!
He's been with me now for oh six
months now, although you know there
are a few things that are bothering

me about my Andre.

He kinda sweats a lot . And
excessive sweat, well it has been
known to turn on you. And I really
don't think he's all that bright
but he tries and he makes me laugh.

So oh well I'll go get the
place all ready. I need to have my
sweaty teddy Andre get busy.

ACT 1

SCENE 3

TIME: 1045:am

MIMI

Entering from stage right..
Andre, where are you Andre?!

ANDRE

Sweeping the vacant room.

Addressing the audience confidentially.
Excuse me now, I must go now, my
Mimi is calling me!

Moves slowly to stage left.

MIMI

Alternating between combing

her hair and cleaning the
bathroom.

I look so good. Someone has
been a
very clean lady. Just look in the
shower, nothing to be seen! And the
place is so clean, look around: no
dirt, no soap scum, not even a
single hair in the shower. No hair
anywhere, Not even one!

ANDRE

Approaching Mimi with confidence
and the strut of a man who knows he
is a stud.
Mimi baby, You are very beautiful.

MIM I
Thank you Andre baby. You arc
beautiful as well.

ANDRE

I know this Darling.

Flexing his muscles and
primping himself in the
mirror.
Now may I shower? I need a
shampooing.

MIMI
Don't move! Don't you move! Look,
look do see what I have in my
hand?!

ANDRE
Sure enough, nasty shower hair.

MIMI

Look in the shower, not a one, not
even one. Removing more hair from her
pocket and holding it up. Look in my hand!
You see, do you

see?
          (Screaming)

Shower hair!
(Suspiciously addressing Andre)

Can it be? Have you broken house
laws? The hair must be yours. There
is no one else here or has been in
quite some time.

Her mood darkens, crazy and paranoid.
So what do you mean by this? You
think I am a bad person?
                    (pause for beat)
Disgusting fallen hair cluttering
up my beautiful Apartment!

ANDRE

Upset and throwing a tantrum.
Noooooo! I can't have this!

He is fighting for mirror time as
he tries to comb his hair.
(pause for beat)
You know, the last time you took in
a border; they were the ones that
caused the mess. The hair must be
left over from them.

MIMI

Raising her voice in a rage
You think that there would be
shower hair in my tub for a whole
week?! Are you out of your mind?!

ANDRE
My hair does not fall out, it is
not allowed to.

Calming down, he looks out at the
audience, and confides his plan.
I have to get someone else, a new
tenant in our vacant room...a nice
young couple of course. I'll get
right on it! I don't want my Mimi
to be mad, at least not at me.

TURNS BACK TO MIMI

MIMI
Inspecting the shower once again.
MIMI
Who are you talking to? You have to
watch that, someone might think
you're not right and lock you up .

ANDRE

Looking in the mirror once again.
(Comforting)
Mimi baby, you know how much I love
you.I know what the problem is, you
are getting bored and lonely since
the Johansons moved out. Well I
will talk to Ralph down the hall,
have him put up some fliers at the
university.

MIMI
(brightening)
Yes, yes, a good idea. It is time.
We do have vacancy, yes, yes...
good thinking.
(pause for beat)
But wait, look again.

Looking in the shower.
(Smugly)

No hair in the shower, not even
one.

ANDRE

Looking in the shower.
That's right baby, not even one.

MIMI
Must keep the place in tip top
condition.

She grabs Andre's cheek, squeezes and exits
the stage.
ANDRE
(To self)
Here we go again.
ACT 1
S CENE 2

TIME: 7:00 am NEXT DAY

SETTING: (CENTER STAGE) RALPH'S
APARTMENT. A BED OR A COUPLE OF
CHAIRS.

AT RISE: RALPH IS SLEEPING. ANDRE IS
KNOCKING ON THE DOOR.

ANDRE
Wake up Ralph, it's Andre. I need
to talk to you! Wake up!

RALPH

Laying in bed, groggy and trying to
ignore Andre. Finally gives up and

rolls out of bed, starts to pull on
his clothes and talks to the door.
I'm trying to sleep...sleeping...
What is it?

ANDRE
You owe Mimi some back rent.

RALPH

Opens the door.
Yes, I do and you will get the
money soon. This is why I need to
sleep, double shifts man, they're
killing me..

ANDRE
Let us work a deal. I need for you
to go out up to the university and
put up posters for a room to rent.

RALPH
(confused)
I just did that a couple of months
ago.

ANDRE
Yeah, well you know, it's time
again.
RALPH
What? Is there an available apt?

ANDRE
Yes, in our place.
RALPH
What happened to the Johansons?

ANDRE
They're gone.
Motioning towards the door.

RALPH

That's strange...

ANDRE
Mimi said they were bad people.

RALPH
Huh, that's funny. They seemed nice
to me... Whatever. How much we
talking?

ANDRE
Ohh, let's see
(pause for beat)
Fifty bucks! And here are the posters.
The sooner the better.

RALPH
O k . Time for coffee. You want some?

ANDRE
No, no, no. I'm like a coffee. You
know my body produces natural
e nergy.I'd say as much as two of
you .

RALPH
Ohh OK then your set,I'll just
have a quick cup.

ANDRE
Find a nice young couple. I will
probably chip away even more on
your rent. As you know, Mimi is
very giving and appreciative..
RALPH
(excitement building)
Don't you worry. I'll get these up
right away.

ANDRE
Gesturing with his hands.

Chip, chip, chip.

RALPH

Finished dressing, he slams his
coffee mug down. His spirits are
high, he is jumping about.
This is great! There's always a
couple out there, who could use a
spot this close to campus.

ANDRE

Moving him along with his
hands in a waving motion.
Off to college you go, off
to
college you go.

RALPH

Getting all of his things together,
preparing to run out the door.
That is where the money is!

ANDRE
Just spread the word a wonderful
place open right next to campus.
Run Ralph r un!

Acting like he is chipping away at

a statue with his hands.

An chip, chip, chip, away your

rent.
Ralph runs out the door
leaving Andre standing
outside.
(pause for beat)

ANDRE

That's right, no worries.

Continually making the gesture
with his hands of having a hammer
and chipping away.
Chip, chip, chip.

Lights down

SCENE 3

Time: 10:15am

SETTING: CENTER STAGE. AN APARTMENT
IN STUDENT HOUSING AT A UNIVERSITY.
THE APARTMENT IS EMPTY EXCEPT FOR
BOXES SCATTERED ABOUT.

AT RISE: RENAY AND JOE ARE PACKING UP BOXES.
PREPARING TO MOVE TO NEW APARTMENT.
RENAY
Packing unpacking. Moving here,
moving there. Seems like we just
got here!

Takes a deep breath,
sighs, finishes packing a
box.
OK, these four boxes and
that's it!

JOE
You should be getting used to it by
now: Kansas, New York, and in two
weeks, Budapest.

RENAY
Yeah, well you know I'll miss you.

JOE

Yeah I know. Three months with the
Gypsy's; you'll have one hell of a
paper to right! Some thesis that
will be.

RENAY
Alright let's not talk about it
today, I'm not leaving for eighteen
more days. Let's get out of this
money pit here!

Packing and talking at the same time.
Can't stay here no siree!
(trying to sound positive)
I'll go to take care of my
requirements for school, you will
stay in a studio apartment off
campus for the summer, then we will
move back in here when school
starts up in the fall.
(pause for beat)
This should work out.
(pause for beat)

Finishes packing and closing up the last box.
That's it. Off to the van! Sure is
nice that Ralph let you use the van
from work.

JOE
Yeah and the good news is we're
done after this trip, only one trip
needed! We have extra room in the
freezer. I took out the ice cream
and set it in a cooler with a bag
of ice so we have to make this trip
fast.

RENAY
Saving us money as usual.

JOE
OK come on, we have to hurry, the
van is due back for the next shift
at four today.

RENAY

Looks at her watch.
Ten thirty. Plenty of time.

JOE
Hold on, let's take one last look
at this place.

Put arms around each other's
shoulders and take one last
look.

LIGHTS DOWN
SCENE 4

TIME 10:45 am

SETTING : CENTER STAGE OUTSIDE OF JOE AND
RENAYS APARTMENT .

AT RISE: JOE AND RENA ARE WALKING
OUT OF THEIR BUILDING TO THE CENTER
OF STAGE. THEY ARE CARRYING HEAVY
BOXE S THEY SIT THEM DOWN.
RENAY

Oh man, that's heavy.
(calmly)
Where is the van?

JOE

Looking up and down the street.
What? It was right here! What the
fuck?!

Slowly getting worked up, he
is starting to get angry.
Damn man, this isn't
happening!
someone has stolen the van.

RENAY

Throwing her hands up in disgust.
All of our things are in there!

Anger is building.
Did you leave the keys in it?!

JOE
Of course not.

Moving back and forth, looking up
and down the street and up at the
signs, panic building.

I need to call the police.

RENAY
Wait a minute. You parked it right
here?
JOE
Yes, right here.

RENAY
Well, look at the sign.

JOE
No parking or you get your van
towed. Is that what you see? I don't!

RENAY
Well look again, No parking on
Wednesday eleven to twelve . Nothing about
getting towed!

Looks at watch.
RENAY
It's 11:02!

JOE
It must have been towed!

RENAY
Let's hope it was towed that way we
can at least get our things back!
JOE
(trying to calm down)
Let me think this out. OK. Why
wouldn't there just be a ticket?

RENAY
There must be outstanding tickets
or something like that!
I can't believe this is happening!
(pause for beat)
I'll call the police.

Dials her cell phone.
Pacing, showing anger at
the situation.

Phone is answered.
Hello Police, I need to report a car
missing. We're not sure if it was
stolen or towed.

JOE

Talking to himself.
This shouldn't be a problem. What,
it can't be more then what, a
hundred dollars? Go down there, get
the van out. It's as simple as
that.

RENAY

Hangs up the phone and walks back
over to Joe and the boxes. You're
not going to believe this.
Not only has all of our things been
taken and towed down to the city tow lot,
they want seven hundred and

something to get it out!

(pause for beat)

And guess what?
(pause for beat)
We don't have it!

JOE
Unpaid tickets? Why is it so much!
I'm going to lose my job over this.

RENAY
What about our things? Fuck your
stupid job! All my books,
everything I own is gone!
(T rying to be calm.)
JOE
I'll go down and try to get our
things.

RALPH

Enters from stage right, very
enthusiastic with fliers in his
hand.
Hey, what's up?
JOE

Motioning over to Renay.
Well, we have a fucking crisis on
our hands, as you can see.

Renay is pacing back and
forth, cursing to herself and
flailing her arms.

JOE

Angry

Do you see the van here?

RENAY
It's not his fault.

JOE

Angrily approaching Ralph.
This is fucked up,they shouldn't
have towed it, a ticket is all
there should be. Were there
outstanding tickets or something
like that?!

RALPH
No, of course not!
(Getting worried.)
Oh shit, oh no. Fuck! You could get
fired for this.

Looks up and down the street
and up at the signs.
JOE
Fired, what the fuck! fuck you!
RENAY
You parked here, what were *you*
thinking!

JOE
And all that ice cream is gonna
melt. I took it out of the ice box
for more room.

RALPH
Where is it?

JOE
I put it in the big beer cooler.
RALPH
You have to pay for that if it
melts!

RENAY

Shut up about the ice cream!
Joey, come here.
There is bad news.
I have to get our things out. I
mean, Jesus, all my books, my
clothes, everything! All we have
left is the deposit money for the
studio.

RALPH
Interrupting and stepping in between the two.

I just finished putting up these
fliers for my landlord for a cheap
room to rent. She'll probably work
with you on the money.

JOE
What, cheaper than a studio?

RENAY
We're going to have to rethink
everything. It was all set up.
Money...gone..Gone!

JOE
I'll get our things and I'll find a
room too. I can stay in, it's only

for the summer.

RENAY
Man, you're really dragging me down.
This is bullshit. You and your
broke ass ways, we should have just
rented a moving truck!
(pause for beat)
But n o, we can't do that, I have to pay
for everything. Sure would be nice
if you could help! Stupid ass,
bullshit job. Wanna be musician,
this sucks! Go... Go... fucking had
it man. Just go! I'll stay at my
friend Mary's house tonight since
we are homeless now!
JOE
Yeah, I'll stay with Ralph tonight.
Is that alright buddy?
RALPH

Sure, no problem.
JOE

Walks over to Renay,
pulls her over to stage
left.
(To Ralph)
Give us a minute.
(To Renay)
Listen, I'll take care of this and
remember, you're leaving in

what

two weeks? So I'll stay in the room
for the summer, I don't mind. You
just focus on preparing for your
trip.I'm sorry this happened, but it

did, so I'll fix it. I promise.

RENAY
I'll see you in the morning. We'll
go look at that place.

JOE
I'll call you from the tow lot.
RENAY
It better be alright. It's all we can afford
now.

LIGHTS DOWN

ACT 2
SCENE 1

TIME: 1:00 pm
SETTING: TICKET WAITING AREA IN THE
TOW LOT, BIG CITY U.S.A. EMPLOYEES
ARE SEATED BEHIND TABLES. PEOPLE
ARE SEATED IN CHAIRS, STANDING,
LEANING AGAINST WALLS, ETC.

AT RISE: JOE AND RALPH WALK INTO THE
TOW LOT. OTHERS ARE SEATED AND
STANDING - WAITING IN LINE.

Joe

Walking in like he owns the place.
This is unbelievable!

TAMERA
S itting behind a desk with a bored
expression.
Take a sit mister. You gotta wait in line
sugar.
RALPH
(Reassuring Joe)
A mistake has been made, it will

all be worked out. I can assure
you.

TRISH
The mistakes just keep coming, is
there no accountability what so
ever around here this whole place
is just one big racket
of thievery.

JOE
Tell me about it lady.

TRISH
It's modern day horse rustling! Hustler's
freaking crooks.

TAMERA
Lady you need to wait your turn.

TRISH
You have no idea what is going on
do you? Huh! I need to talk to the
Captain dammit!
TAMERA

Pathetic, something stinks in here!
JOE
The whole place stinks.
(To Tamera)
Listen to me I need
this money! What is this? There was
no reason to tow the car and then
want all of this money, there has
to be a mistake!

TAMERA
Sir, I told you to sit down there
with all the other mistakes
and I'll get to you. Damn! What you
just off the boat son? We have

order up in here, order.

JOE
Alright, OK, I understand: wait in
line not out of order.

TAMERA
Good, you catch on quick.
(Loud)
Next! Lilly Smiles where you at,
Lilly Smiles.

LILLY

Quickly wakes up where she is
seated with everyone else. Yes
I'm the Lilly, someone tell me
what's going on!

TRISH
(seated beside Lilly)
You're not from around here are
you honey?

LILLY
No. To be honest with you, I just
woke up and a guard told me to come
in here. I'm still in New York
right?

TRISH
Ohhhh yeah. What are you smoking?
TAMERA
You say don't know how you got
here?

LILLY
I must have been lost,I drove up
from Vermont for the Sheryl Crow
Concert.
(Suddenly worried.)

Did I miss it?
(Remembering)
I asked for directions. To Madison
Square Garden and this kid told me
I was "in Bushwick Bitch!"

RALPH
Ohh that is nowhere near the
garden!

LILLY
I figured that out.

JOE
So your car got towed in from
Brooklyn?

LILLY
No, I finally made it over to the
Arena. Decided to park for the
night, get some shuteye.

RALPH
So, how'd your car get towed?

LILLY
I went to sleep in my back camper
shell. Next thing I know, I'm here.

TRISH
(Amazed)
So you just slept through the
tow!?

LILLY
Yeah, I woke up here in the
garage.

JOE
This is unbelievable. I feel like
I'm in the Twilight Zone!

TRISH
Ohhhh you're in the zone alright,
t he t ow z one!

LILLY
Oh you said twilight zone this is
heavy, to heavy for me you two go
ahead. I'll be over here listening
to some Sheryl Crow.
P uts headphones on. S inging as she goes back
to sit down.

LILLY
If it makes you happy.

Trish
You know you disgust me all hipped
out, Not a care in the world. Must
be nice!

LILLY
If it makes you happy.

T RISH
Get the Captain in here now.
JOE
Lady please! my life is tinkering
towards total madness.

JOE

M oving towards the officer's table
I have to get my things out!
(To Ralph)
Why is it so much?

RALPH
That's just the way it is I guess.
You were in a handicap zone or
something.

JOE
That's crazy! There were no signs
that said that. Well it's the company's fault
for
not paying the outstanding tickets!
RALPH
Stop saying that. I told you there
are no tickets other then the one
you got.
(Letting Joe in on a secret.)
Well, you're new here my friend.
The signs say whatever they want
them to say.

JOE
What are you talking about?! There
has got to be a sign posted some
where!

RALPH
I don't know man, maybe there used
to be a sign there. Who freaking
knows? This is New York!

JOE
We have no choice. When we get to
the front of the line, we will talk
to the guard and straighten this
all out and get my money back.

RALPH
Sounds good to me! Just talk to the
nice lady behind the bullet proof
window there. I'm sure she will
hook you right up.

JOE
Alright then, that's what I'll do.
She looks nice enough to me.

RALPH
I'm sure she is.

JOE
Well OK, I hope it will work out.

RALPH
This will all work out in the end.
And besides, look at it like this;
you will have very, very cheap rent
now that you're moving in over by me.

JOE

That's not the deal. I'm not spending this
money.
They made the mistake, not
me.
RALPH
Oh I know, I was just saying, in
case they decide to be difficult.
(C ondescending)
Yes, yes, yes;
this should work .

JOE
Look around and see all the angry people.

RALPH
We have to get the van out now! If
my Uncle finds out about you taking
all the ice cream out and using it
as storage space, then getting the
freaking car towed, he is sure to
fire you and he's going to kick my
ass!

TAMERA
Step back behind the red line sir,
wait until you are called

JOE
You don't understand. Everything I
own is in the van. You guys made a
mistake.

TAMERA

Laughing very loud.
So, what: you're homeless?

JOE
No, we were moving.

TAMERA
That's a new one. Hahahaha!
Get back in line.

JOE

Gets back in line
Okay, Okay.

(pause for beat)

TAMERA
Ralph Ozzie, paging Ralph Ozzie!
RALPH

Jumps up.

Yes, thank you! My ice cream truck?

TAMERA
Your ice cream truck is ready. That
will be seven hundred and eighty
six dollars.
Driver's License, insurance, and
money and you can go check on your
ice cream.

JOE

Moving up towards the guard window.
Hey Lady, I wanted to talk to you.
There seems to be a mistake with
the towing of this van.

TAMERA
(S houting)
Behind the red line! Am I going to
have to call a guard up in here? I
said step back to the red line.
I'll get to it when I can!

JOE
My god, you don't have to yell.

TAMERA
Is your name Ralph Ozzie?
JOE
No.
TAMERA
Then step back behind the red line
until I call your name.

JOE
(D esperate)
But you don't understand! There has
been a mistake with Ralph's Van, it
shouldn't have been towed. There
were no signs saying tow zone.
TAMERA

Well in that case, hold everything.
Let me help you. Tamera looks down
at her computer.
(Pause for beat)

TAMERA

Nope. Says right here "van parked
in a handicap zone".

RALPH
There wasn't a sign.

JOE
I swear there was no sign !

TAMERA
Drivers license, proof of
insurance, seven hundred and eighty
six dollars, or take it up with the
judge.
Defeated, Joe gives Ralph the money

RALPH

Hands over the money to Tamera.
Alright, here.

TAMERA
Here is your receipt. Just go
outside, follow the signs to check
out your vehicle.
(Pause for beat)

And have a nice day.

Ralph and Joe exit stage right.

Pat and Irene enter from stage
right. Irene is sweeping, Pat is
picking up trash

PAT
This is my favorite part of the
job.
Hey Tamera, how are you?

TAMERA
Is it just me or is there something

a little stank in here?

PAT
(N onchalantly)
There's a body in a hearse in the
back.

Pat stops picking up trash.

TAMERA
What, you kidding right?

PAT
Call up the Captain. This is a
mistake. Call the Captain! This is
a tow lot, not a dam morgue.

TAMERA
We can't let the Captain know about
this. Didn't you check the car when
it was brought in?!

PAT
I thought I did. I was checking in
and ..

In walks Captain Mondo from stage right.
CAPTAIN MONDO
Stink, what's that I hear about
stink? Pick up this trash.

P oin ts at some trash.
Damn, it smells like ass in here.
You obviously have been slacking.
This place is a mess!

PAT
We have a situation..
That smell isn't from the trash.

CAPTAIN MONDO
Pat, what are you talking about?
PAT
What she means to say sir, is that
there is a body in a hearse in the
back garage.

CAPTAIN MONDO
Well that is a problem. Call the
driver, get it the hell out of
hear.

PAT
There is no record of a tow in sir.
CAPTAIN MONDO
Well how did it get here?
You know what, forget about it,
I'll take care of the dead guy.
PAT
Yes sir.
CAPTAIN MONDO
(To Tamera)
Back up from the front
office! We have a code yellow.
No one is allowed in the back until
I tell you otherwise.

TAMERA
What's going on?

CAPTAIN MONDO
This shouldn't take long. Stall
anyone from leaving and you know
the drill; stall, stall, stall.

TRISH
Excuse me I represent Finelli's
Fine Funerals

TAMERA

What in line Missy!

TAMERA
Yes sir, I know the drill.
Don't worry sir.

CAPTAIN MONDO
I'll send up one of the guards if
this ends up taking longer then 10
minutes.

TRISH

Approach es the desk.
Excuse me, are you people freaking
deaf.I represent Finelli's Fine
Funerals and one of our cars I have
been told is here.

TAMERA
You're going to have to wait in
line ma'am.
CAPTAIN MONDO
No, no it's alright, let her in.
TAMERA
Yes sir.
CAPTAIN MONDO
You leave something in one of your car's.

TRISH
Are there any limits on the depths
of humanity your drivers will not
stoop to make a buck? The driver
had a heart attack in the middle of
the funeral recession. Then the
car, as you can see, hit the
m edian. You were *supposed* to take the body
out and take the casket to the
cemetery. Obviously some one fucked
up!

CAPTAIN MONDO
Just get it out of here!

TRISH
You tow guys, greedy motherfuckers,
you'd tow your own mama for a buck,
wouldn't you!?

LIGHTS DOWN

ACT 2

SCENE 2

TIME 1:45 pm
SETTING: 6TH FLOOR WALK UP APARTMENT, INSIDE
THE BUILDING

AT RISE: JOE AND RENAY ARE OUTSIDE
OF THE APARTMENT TALKING TO WHO THEY
THINK ARE THE OWNERS OF THE BUILDING
ABOUT RENTING A ROOM FOR A FEW
MONTHS.
MIMI
Who is it?
Talk's through the door.
We're friends of Ralph. I'm Joe,
with my girlfriend Renay; we're here
about the apartment.

RENAY
S haking hands with Mimi.
Nice to meet you.

MIMI
Andre, come in here
and meet this nice
young couple.
ANDRE
Hello!

S haking both of their hands with both of his
hands.

JOE
So when we talked, you said this
was a good time to come by?

MIMI
Of course! Let me show you around
the place.

M oving gracefully and
extending her arm inside like
a showroom model.
JOE AND RENAY
(They enter the apartment.)

MIMI
Here is our wonderful living room
and are kitchen with microwave and
full use is included with the room.
You do share the bathroom but as
you can see it is immaculate. We
like to keep it that way, nice and
sparkling.

ANDRE
I like to watch her show the place.

RENAY
Ohh that's sweet.

JOE
This is great.
MIMI
So Renay, you are a student at the
university?

RENAY
Yes, I'm leaving for the summer to

do research for my thesis and we
thought we could save some money by
getting out of student housing for
the summer. We had a little bad
luck with finances lately that's
why we're in such a short notice
situation here.

MIMI
Oh yes I understand, things do
happen. I do think you will be more
than comfortable here.

RENAY
This is very nice. I'll be here for about two
and a half weeks.
Joe would like to stay for the
summer then we'll go back to
student housing. This seems
perfect.

MIMI
Oh yes, we often have students from
the university.

RENAY
Do you have an application form or
lease for us to look over.

ANDRE
Yes, I'll be right back with the
forms.

MIMI
Wait, we only have six month leases.

JOE
Oh no! That's too bad, we're only
looking for 3 months.

MIMI

Well I'll tell you what, excuse me
for a minute, let me talk to my
Andre for a moment.
They turn away and start talking quietly.

ANDRE

A cting excited !
Is the race on?

JOE
L ooking over at Renay then to Mimi.
What race?

MIMI
Oh, there is no race. No hurry whatsoever.

ANDRE
T have things to fix.

E xits.

MIMI
You can do a month to month, how
does that sound?

RENAY
That's perfect! so the lease.

Andre enters with papers in his hands.

ANDRE
Here you go! The papers, right
here.

MIMI
Thank you baby.

ANDRE
L ooking over at Joe.
Remember. I get the red car this
time.

MIMI
You sure do.

ANDRE
Sure enough, Sure enough,

JOE
You're getting a car?

MIMI
Yes, a red Mustang. He has always
wanted one.

ANDRE
Mustang-red. Sure enough, sure
e nough!
RENAY
Cool.
JOE
O k, then we will be right back.

MIMI
Alright,   around
what time? I want
to make sure I'm
here to give you
the key.

RENAY
Well, probably around an hour.

JOE
That's alright isn't it?

MIMI
Well you never know,
someone else might
be by. Could you
leave a deposit?

JOE
OK, here is half,
I'll bring the rest
in an hour. Could
you give me a
receipt?

ANDRE
Here is the receipt.

JOE
(Mildly surprised)
Ok then, thanks.
We'll see you
soon.
ANDRE
Thank you.

(Pause for beat)
Thank you very much.

ACT 2
SCENE 3

Time: 3:30pm
SETTING: IN THE STAIRWELL OF MIMI'S
APARTMENT.
AT RISE: JOE AND RENAY ARE BRINGING IN BOXES.
RENAY IS STRUGGLING WITH A LARGE BOX.

MIMI
Ohh goodness, let me help you with
that.

RENAY
Thank you! That's so sweet of you.

MIMI
Of course, I do enjoy helping the

needy.

They walk into the room.
I want to talk to you about these
beautiful curtains.

RENAY
They're kind of retro, don't you
think Joey?

JOE
Yeah, I get that feel.

MIMI
Yes, these curtains are quite retro
made, I do mean homemade, stitched
thread by thread by my late great
Grandmother. You know she lived
here in this very room for Ohh, I
don't know, twenty years or so.

RENAY
That's so sweet. So you took good
care of her and she was able to be
around her loved ones, that's
great, just great.

JOE
Whew! That's about it.
(Pause for beat.)
Is it hot in here?

RENAY
Yeah it is.

JOE
Yesterday, it was nice and cool in
here.

RENAY
Feels like the heat's on.
(Pause for beat)
It is, feel the pipes.

JOE

T ouch ing the pipes.
Open the window!

RENAY

T rying to open the window.
It won't open!

JOE
Let me go talk to Mimi. I'm sure
they can fix this.

Renay continues to try and open the
window. She notices that the window
is nailed shut. Leaves to get Joe.
(Pause for beat.)

Joe and Renay enter stage

JOE
That's funny, he's gone. He
was just here.

RENAY
Well, leave the door open.

You're not going to believe this.
RENAY
What?
JOE
Look at the window, it's nailed
shut.

JOE

Well, we'll just have to have Andre
fix it so we can put our air
conditioner in. It's fucking
August.
M IMI
E nters apartment with Andre behind her. He is
playing with an electric red toy car.

ANDRE
All moved in?

JOE
Yes.

Excuse me, do you know this window
is nailed shut?

MIMI

G oes over to the
window, looks at it
surprised.
This is strange?

JOE
We want to put our air conditioner
in.

MIMI
Andre come here. Quit playing with
your car for a moment.

ANDRE
S ets controls down on the floor.
Is there a problem?

JOE
We can't get the window opened.

MIMI
Huh, that's weird. You know what?

The last guy to rent
this place must have done that. He
was always worried about someone
breaking in.

RENAY
(Very politely)
And why is the heat on in here?

MIMI
(S uddenly hostile)

No reason to get snotty with me!

RENAY
I'm just asking.

MIMI

P leasant again.

This is news to me, there must be
a problem with the boiler. It's
only on in this room
h ow peculiar.

ANDRE
I'll get right on it.

Picks up his toy car controller and starts
playing with it.

MIMI
Should be fixed soon; until then,
come on out here, it's cool out
here.

RENAY
I have to leave for class. Have to
get cleaned up, take a shower. Joe,
help me find the shampoo.

MIMI
Ohhh make sure you use conditioner
and a hair net. Don't leave any
hair in the shower princess.

RENAY

Gathering some of her clothes and a towel.
Alright.

JOE
I'll make dinner honey.

MIMI
What, you have food here?

JOE
Yes, we brought some food from our
house.

R ENAY
Tries to walk out of the room, Mimi
discreetly steps in her way.
RENAY
Excuse me.
MIMI
Remember what I said, don't leave
the bathroom messy.

Renay walks by and exits the stage.

ANDRE
Hahahahhaha! Look how fast my car
goes! Weeeee!

JOE
Is he gonna fix the heat in here,
and the window?

MIMI
What? Are you trying to cause

trouble? I told you the pipes in
here are broken.

JOE
Well OK, then how about the window
so we can put our air conditioner
in?

MIMI
Are you ok?

JOE
What do you mean?

MIMI
Don't you remember? We told you the
air conditioner out here in the
hallway is the only air conditioner
the circuit breakers can handle.

JOE
You never said that.

MIMI
Oh that's right, I told your
princess. She must have forgotten
to tell you. You know if I were
you, I'd watch her.

JOE
I'm going to the kitchen.

M IMI
B locks the doorway. She presses up
against him, he tries to avoid
her.
MIMI
Watch your hands young man.
JOE
What?
JOE

You heard me, my Andre is very
jealous.

ANDRE
Hahahaha! What did I hear,
"jealous"? Are you jealous of my
car? It's mine, mine, mine. You
should feel privileged just to look
at it.

JOE
Whatever, I'm going to the kitchen.

Notices the door right next to his, pauses.
So you two live in this room? I
thought that door was a closet. You
didn't open it when we were here
before.

MIMI
I told you we lived here. The ad
said room for rent in apartment.
We're right down the hall.

JOE
Pointing at their door.
Yeah, a whole two feet.

Walks down the hall to the kitchen

MIMI
(T o Andre)
We got a trouble maker here.

ANDRE
Trouble? You want me to get your
cousins?

MIMI
No, not yet. Why don't you pretend
to do something around here?

ANDRE
Yeah, that's a good idea.
(L ouder)
ANDRE
OK good, then I have to go now. I
need to go fix light bulb in D2.
And paint the flowers.

E XIT STAGE LEFT .
MIMI

Walks down the hall to the
kitchen seductively singing.
Somebody's gonna hur t
  someone,
while the heat is on! Some body's
gonna hurt someone, while the heat
is on! Ohh Ohh , some body's gonna
hurt someone, while the heat is
on!

JOE
You like to sing huh?

MIMI
Oh yeah, you like my voice?

RENAY

Enters stage, dressed for
school with books in hand
Was that you? I thought I
heard
singing, sounded pretty good.

JOE
Oh good your out! Excuse me, nature
calls.

EXITS

MIMI
Thank you. I was just telling your
boyfriend that you need to move
your things out of the kitchen.

RENAY
Why what's wrong? Has something
happened?

MIMI
It seems that some of your open
boxes of dry goods, which by the
way you should know better little
lady, do you want there to be a bug
infestation?
RENAY
Well we just moved in, some of the
boxes must have gotten knocked
around.

MIMI
Is that what you do?

RENAY
What do you mean? knock around?

MIMI
You know, kind of get around?

RENAY
I'm not sure what you mean by that
but yes, we have moved around quite
a bit these past few years.

MIMI
Alright then, can you move these
boxes out of here?

RENAY
You said we could keep some of our
food in the kitchen when we rented

the room.
MIMI
No!
RENAY
OK, that's alright. I guess we can
make room in our room.

MIMI
Thank you. Don't want to get bugs,
that's nasty.

RENAY
Well all my things here are sealed.
Can't you see that?

MIMI
No, I've seen some open boxes.

RANEY
Since when, we just moved in
today?

ANDRE

Enters back on stage.
Look baby, see how fast my car
goes! Electric car toy yeah!

MIMI

Jumping up and down.
Go, make it go fast, fast!

RENAY

Starts picking up boxes from the kitchen.
I'll move these things.

MIMI
Ohh you don't have to do that now.
Can't you see Andre wants to play
in here now?

ANDRE
Ha, ha, go, go!

RENAY
Alright, I'll take care of it after
class.

MIMI
Whatever. That's fine.

RENAY

Knocks on the bathroom door.
Hey Joe, I'm going to class, see
you tonight.
Oh by the way, when I get home,
can you help me in the kitchen?

JOE
Sure, with what?

RENAY
Well, seems like we have to move
all of our things into our room.

JOE

Comes out of the bathroom, looks
over at the kitchen and sees Mimi
and Andre playing.
What? Why?
RENAY
Something about bugs.
MIMI

Mimi gets out a pair of white
gloves and is putting them on as
Andre watches.

ANDRE
(Excited)

Misses clean, misses clean!

MIMI
(T o Renay)
You didn't wash your clothes in the
tub did you?

RENAY
Listen lady, I think you have me
confused with someone else.

MIMI
What do you mean?

RENAY
Well, someone who will put up with
your mouth! We rent a room from you
that is it. You're not to get in my
face about every little thing that
goes on around here. Your knit
picking wasn't included in the
lease I signed so back the fuck
off! You are fucking with the wrong
person!

MIMI
There better not be any hair in
that shower!

RENAY

E xits stage.

I'm leaving now.
ANDRE

S till playing with his toy car.
ANDRE
Check it out. Cool, huh?

JOE
Sure, real cool.

ANDRE
Ohhh you know it, ain't that right
Mimi? My car is the coolest.

MIMI
That's right. You like his car
don't you Joe?

JOE
Yeah sure.

MIMI
So what are you
 gonna do about this
crap your girlfriend
left all over the
place!?
JOE
What crap?
MIMI

This open box. The bugs will come.
I can't have open sugar, it's
dirty. She said she'd take care of this,
where is she?
JOE
She went to class.
ANDRE
Somebody's in trouble.
JOE

Don't worry about it. I'll take
care of it right now. Don't want
any problems.
MIMI
Ooh don't worry, no problems.

ANDRE

Raising his head.
Somebody's in trouble.

JOE
I have to go to work. I can throw
all of this in a box for now and
put it in our room ok?

MIMI
OK, that's fine. Thank you. You
really should talk with your
girlfriend.

JOE
Can I ask you a question?

MIMI
Sure baby.

ANDRE

Drops his controller and
speed walks out the door.
I have to go.

JOE
When we moved in, you said we had
use of the kitchen.

MIMI
Sure did, you can use it all you
want. But don't leave any food or
dishes out here.

JOE
Oh, I must have misunderstood.

MIMI
It's your girlfriend, she's kind of
messy.

JOE
Okay.

Starts putting food in box.

MIMI

Looking at Joe like a piece of
white meat on thanksgiving. Takes
off her gloves.
But you're nice an tight.
(Pause for beat.)
I mean tidy.

ANDRE

Enters yelling in English and broken Russian.
Plumbing, the Upstairs, Mimi- now
now, now, Russian rambling...

JOE

Picks up box walks out.
I got it all. I gotta go to work
bye.

Puts box in his room and walks out the door.

ANDRE
As he exits grabs plunger and tools.
This is getting into my racing
time. Be back later.

MIMI

Walks over to his car and
smashes it with her feet
Don't interrupt me, never
interrupt me. Never interrupt me! I'll smash
you
dead.

Calms down and becomes completely
silent. Walks over to the broom and
dust pan and grabs a trash bag,
sweeps up the toy car then puts it
in the bottom of the trash bag.
Never interrupt me!
(Pause for beat.)

Notices what she has done and calms down.
I can't believe someone has
stolen my man's new car.
(Pause for beat.)
This is terrible, just terrible.
And ohh my god, this place is a
d isaster.
Puts her white gloves back on and starts
cleaning.
A NDRE
S tarts cutting at the mop head in
his hands.
LIGHTS DOWN

SCENE 4

TIME: 9:30 pm

Setting: Mimi's apartment. A
dark room lit only by a
small light.

AT RISE: MIMI IS SITTING ON A CHAIR.
SHE IS WEARING A ROBE AND WHITE
GLOVES AND HOLDING A BALL OF HAIR.
ANDRE HAS A MOP IN HIS HAND AND A
PAIR OF SCISSORS. HE IS PACING AND
CUTTING THE EXCESS MOP STRINGS.

ANDRE

It is getting late! I have evened the mop
head. You
like?

MIMI
That's nice. Is that what you
learned from that slut Sasha, how
to even the mop on her nasty head?

ANDRE
You should not talk of Sasha that
way. She had a beautiful head of hair.

MIMI
She was a dirty bitch if you ask
me.

ANDRE
Mimi you are tired and cranky, you
don't mean to be. I now have a question for
you.
What happened to my car?

MIMI
Like I told you, the new dirty
haired tenant has taken your
precious possession.
ANDRE
No repo man in this house, it's not
a llowed.
ANDRE
No, no.
MIMI
This isn't a tow zone either.

MIMI
Of course not baby. Don't you worry
now, come here an sit down next to
M e.
ANDRE

Andre slides over and sits at Mimi's feet.
(Pause for beat)
You do know there might be a chance
those two criminals pawned your car
for drugs.

ANDRE
Slamming his mop down on the floor.
Oh no, don't say that. Not again!

MIMI
Baby, you know how they are.

ANDRE
They're jealous of us, everyone is.

MIMI
That's right, and look in my hand,

She opens up her hand. It has
wet shower hair in it, it's
hanging from her glove.
H air in the shower makes me frown!

(Hysterical)
I said, hair in the shower makes me
frown!

A NDRE
G ets up and tries to calm her down.
MIMI

Pushing Andre off of her.
Thieves and d irty tenants, we
can't have this, they have to go!
You know, we'll have to keep their
deposit. There is all this damage.
L ooking in her hand at the hairs.

RENAY

Walks in.

LIGHTS UP ALL THE WAY. FLASHING ON
AND OFF FAST AS THEY CAN FOR 4
BEATS.

Andre and Mimi start to move towards Renay.

RENAY
Hey Mimi, listen. I wanted to
apologize, I think we got off to a
bad start.

MIMI
Oh noooo, we're just getting started,
Princess.
Holding up a hand full of hair.
What is this, how is this, and why
is this?

RENAY
You're fucking crazy, what the fuck
is your problem?I'm going to my
room.

Walks over to the door, the key doesn't work.
ANDRE
Why'd you steal my car, are you
dope fiend?

RENAY
Your car? Why would I want a stupid
toy car?

My key isn't working.
MIMI
(To Andre)
She pawned it for drugs!

RENAY

I don't do drugs and you're
starting to scare me. I mean
serious, you're scaring me. Why is
my key not working dammit?

MIMI
You're liars and thieves, you get
no second chance with me! You
aren't allowed in your room, until
Joe comes home, you have to stay
out here with me.

RENAY
Calm down lady, please. We can work
this out, I'm sorry about the hair
in the shower, I'll clean it up.
Why are you doing this? Please
stop.

MIMI
You know Andre, Renay is a lot like
Sasha!

ANDRE
Sasha, why do you talk of Sasha?
MIMI
Andre, Sasha left you just like
Renay is leaving Joe - the same
way, cheating with drug dealers as
well.

ANDRE
Really, you do this?

Moving towards Renay with the mop in his
hands.

RENAY
Put the mop down.

ANDRE

Unscrews the mop head
and holds it like a
spear.
Where is my car?
RENAY
I'll buy you another car!

MIMI
Pointing at Renay.
She's just like Sash! "When you went to work
Joe, she was
here and I saw her with another
man. She's a dirty nasty person."

RENAY
Fuck you lady, you off your meds?
Freaking whack job!

MIMI
You have to leave-you can't stay
here, leave, leave!

RENAY
Tries to get into her room again.
MIMI

Holds scissors up like a barber

and makes a couple of snips in

the air.
MIMI
I will let you stay here, just let
me cut your hair Renay. It's a
simple solution to the problem.
Come here honey, come on, come on,
here kitty, kitty.

RENAY
(Screaming)
Get the fuck out of my way! I'm

leaving. Help, help, someone help
me!

Panicking, Renay desperately tries
to open her door. She stops and
runs away toward the front door.
She pushes past Mimi and Mimi
falls to the floor.

MIMI
(Screaming)

Don't let her leave! She has your car!
ANDRE

He grabs Renay as she runs past, he
trips and they fall to the ground.
Renay is scratching at the door,
barely reaching the knob. Andre is
fighting with her.

M IMI
S tands up and pulls out a little
double duce derringer that she has
in a garter holster around her
thigh. She walks over, calmly
reaches down and shoots one shot at
Reney then leans down and talks to
Andrea for 15 seconds then shoots
him l ike someone who has done this
before.

BANG!

Andre dies instantly.
MIMI
She leans over and kneels behind
the two bodies. She grabs the

scissors and a towel and starts
cutting Renay's hair.

RENAY
Lays unconscious but still alive.
She is looking at the gun on the
floor beside her.

MIMI
My little lady, you have made such
a mess. It's that time again, a
good spring cleaning is in order.
You two be still now. You need a
haircut.
I'll take care of you
honey. Andre you two running off
together back to Europe? Ahh... I
understand, to study abroad, it is
romantic.

Alrighty then Andre, let me get you
ready for your trip.

(Dragging him out)
Andre, I have known for some time
now that you have been homesick. I
just hope the two of you will be
happy together.

Drops Andre off stage. She takes

of

wallet and cell phone of

Renay.

You won't be needing these. I'll
be right back to help you prepare
for your trip.

She grabs the mop and starts moping

b
e
h
i
n
d

t
h
e

t
w
o

o
f

t

LIGHTS DOWN
(Pause for beat.)
L IGHTS HALFWAY BACK UP.
There is blood all over her white
gloves. There is some sort of cart
with wheels and two big trash bags
filled with body parts.

MIMI
Hi hoe, hi hoe, it's off to the
incinerator we go. Hi hoe, hi hoe,
hi hoe, hi hoe, hi hoe, hi hoe.

Throws one of the bags behind a
curtain on the other side of stage.
I do believe the boiler is working
ohh so well.
Ohh one more bag of nasty into the
incinerator.

She throws her white gloves in as
well and then immediately puts on a
new pair.
Now I have to get back upstairs to
my lovely apartment. It's so dirty
down here in the basement. I
mustn't keep Renay waiting.
(Pauses for beat)
Eww..it smells down here.

I have to make things look good
clean and fresh.
It's nice you know, my goal has
always been to recreate that
country fresh smell.
My lovely Joey Joe will be home
soon and you know he will be upset
about what's-her-name running off
with Andre.

It's so sad. I'll have to show him
the letter, the goodbye letter
(Crying out)

MIMI
Ohh the humanity!
My poor, poor Jocy, my new sweetie
pie. Joey my, my poor, poor Joey.

There is so much to do. He will be
heartbroken as I am sure to be as
well.

(Pause for beat)

Although I do believe he will be so
happy to know that he can stay here
rent free from now on. Since I feel
somewhat responsible for all that
has happened.
LIGHTS DOWN
SCENE 5

Time: 10:15pm

SETTING: Mimi's apartment, inside the front
door

AT RISE: Renay wakes up.

There is a little blood on the side

o
f

h
e
r

h
e
a
d
.

RENAY

She crawls over to the door and
can't get it open so she crawls
to other side of the stage

RENAY
My keys are gone, my phone..
(Visibly upset)

Ohh God, please help me! Think,
think... Ok, I have to hide.

Hiding in the shower..

On her way she grabs the mop handle
and takes off the tip so it's only
a pointed end now.
Crying, stop, think- I gotta get
help I'm bleeding...
She rips her shirt off to use as a bandage for
her head. Don't go into shock, weapon, hide.

She crawls behind the shower
curtain to hide just in nick
of time.

(Pause for beat)

Breathing heavy, she begins
slowing down her breathing.
MIMI
Enters the room and
locks the door behind
herself.
Oh my, where have you
gone? My
little wanderer, I thought for sure
you would be resting for your trip.
I wonder, where have you gone?

She pulls out her double deuce
 derringer again and puts in
another round.
Well the good news is, I have
another round for the little lady.

She walks around the stage slowly.
Here kitty, kitty, here kitty. You
need to start packing sweetie.

Andre 's already packed an waiting
for you.

Aww.... hiding in the shower are
we?

Pulls the shower curtain back
and points gun at Renay.

RENAY
Stabs at Mimi and knocks the gun
out of her hand. She is
screaming, hysterical, and crying
at the same time.
Leave me alone!

Throws Mimi down to the ground.
She holds her there using the mop
handle. She reaches down and
grabs the gun.
RENAY
(ANGRY)
Don't you move you sick fucking
bitch. Don't move or I swear I will
stab you and shoot you in the face.

MIMI
This isn't right...

RENAY
Shut up! Don't move. You're sick,
you need help.

MIMI

S tarts to ball up into a fetus position.
(Crying)

This is not how it works.
No, no, this isn't right.

RENAY

Renay grabs her phone out of Mimi's pocket.

Shut up!
MIMI
(C rying)

This isn't right.
RENAY
(Yelling, angry!)
You destroy lives! How many people
have you done this to right? Right?
What do you know about right? You're
not right.

M IMI
Reverting to childlike behavior.
I'll be good I'll be good this inst
the way things are supposed to be.
I'll be good, Mommy I'll be good.
RENAY

Dials the cell phone keeping the
gun on Mimi at all times.
Joe bring the police! Come home!
Come home! Help, please come home
now!

Mimi slowly becomes quieter and
quieter until you only hear a quiet
cry.
LIGHTS DOWN

www.ingramcontent.com/pod-product-compliance
Lightning Source LLC
Chambersburg PA
CBHW051349150726
48000CB00003B/1113